I0784303

WHISPERS IN THE DARK

AN ANTHOLOGY

COMPILED BY

TENITA C. JOHNSON

Published by So It Is Written, LLC
Detroit, MI
SoItIsWritten.net

Whispers in the Dark: An Anthology
Copyright © 2024 by Tenita C. Johnson

Edited by: So It Is Written – www.SoItIsWritten.net

Formatting: Ya Ya Ya Creative – YaYaYaCreative@gmail.com

ISBN: 979-8-9912588-1-4

LCCN: 2024915961

PRINTED AND BOUND IN THE UNITED STATES OF AMERICA

Visionary Author Statement

TENITA C. JOHNSON

For four weeks, Avondale Middle School students worked to study the art of creative writing. During our time together, the students not only engaged in creative writing prompts weekly, and writing sprints, but they also had the chance to collaborate to compile this project. The students had to choose the theme of the book in which they wanted to publish as a group project and, as you can see, they agreed to write stories in the horror/fantasy genre.

In addition to choosing the topic, students were given the task of writing their 1,500-word story by a strict deadline. They also had to read their stories several times aloud in class weekly for feedback from their peers. In addition, the students learned how to self-edit and edit others' work. They did not edit just based on spelling, grammar and punctuation; they also had to edit the stories for consistency, tone, voice, creativity and storyline. Finally, the students worked together to choose a cover image that they all loved for the final front cover.

What you see here today is a product of weeks of hard work, dedication and consistency from students who had a passion to complete a pivotal project in such a short time. Some are fictional, while others are based on their own life experiences. While many students started the class, these are the twelve students who were dedicated to getting to the finish line. I want to personally thank the Avondale School District staff and the students' parents for ensuring that they showed up for the program consistently and finished strong.

The stories you are about to read are a full reflection of their creativity and artistic genius. Enjoy the following stories as these students take you into their worlds of horror or fantasy, or a combination of the two. Keep reading, if you dare!

Tenita "Bestseller" Johnson

Table of Contents

I Wish to be Great

EVELYN YOUNG

Marie sits at her desk, papers all around her with only the light from the lamp sitting next to her. All her co-workers had already left. It was shortly after midnight. She's always been like this: indulged in her work and nothing else. Her colleagues view her as cold and rude due to her snappy attitude. Marie never took time to get to know anyone or build relationships. She deemed it unnecessary. She looked up at the clock, squinting to make out the numbers in the dimly lit room. She takes a deep breath and begins to pack up her stuff, making sure she doesn't leave any papers behind before heading towards the door.

It's 1958. She is the only woman in her field. Sure, there are other women working for the company. But they are all secretaries or simple calculators. Even with the highest IQ between her colleagues, Marie was looked down upon for being a woman. She learned through the countless nights of staying awake when she was studying as a child that being top of her class, skipping multiple grades, and still not being recognized for how smart she was, was almost exhausting. The only way she could be seen as great is if she accomplished something no man had. Something the world has only ever seen in fiction movies, something that everyone thought was impossible.

Marie walks down the long hallways of her workplace, almost silent, not for her footsteps eventually leading her to the exit. She opens the door, stepping out of the building into the parking lot behind her place of work. Only one car is parked: a 1956 black Buick Roadmaster. Right after graduating college, Marie decided that it was in her favor to get a car before she started her job. She already had a driver's license. She had gotten one as soon as she could. It's just, at that age, Marie didn't want to spend her money on a car until she was financially stable. It's not like her parents were going to help pay for it; they wouldn't want to waste money on their daughter. After all, she's a woman. What would she need a car for? Plus, she hadn't minded taking the bus.

Marie placed her belongings in the passenger seat next to her before starting up the car. She puts on her seatbelt, checks her mirror, backs up the car, and drives away. The sky is full of stars as the moon is big and bright; what a beautiful night.

Marie walks through the back doors, the same doors that she'd left the night prior. She walks down the same hallway from before, carrying the same papers, in the same bag. She meets the door to the lab and walks in. Inside, she sees some of her colleagues are already there: Bob, Jim and her boss Dan.

"Hey, good morning, Marie!" Dan exclaims as soon as he notices her presence.

"Good morning, Dan," Marie replies before heading to her desk and placing down her bag.

Dan had always been the only one who didn't look down on her. Whenever other male colleagues made a passive aggressive comment relating to her being a woman, he would always stand up for her. Even if she doesn't show it, she feels deeply for him. She was grateful to at least have one person see her for more than her gender.

Jim doesn't say anything. Jim has found that whenever he tries to speak to Marie, she doesn't just fawn over him. She simply ignores the sexist jokes he makes. Perhaps he remains silent because he knows Dan will call him out if he says anything along those lines. Bob doesn't greet Marie either. He just glances at Jim, then back at his work. He normally just laughs at Jim's jokes. It's obvious he just does so to be a part of his group. Even when Bob knows what Jim does is wrong, he never speaks up or steps in. Too scared. What a coward.

Marie opens her bag, taking out papers covered front to back with her work. One piece of paper had a specific formula written on it. The formula was circled with writing beside it. It read, "Our chance to be great." Like I mentioned before, Marie wishes to be great. She wants people to remember her, Marie Watson, for being an amazing scientist that did the undoable. You see, Marie has dedicated her work to being the first to create a drug that increases a person's strength, speed and smarts. Marie believes that she has finally found it. This formula will transform the average person into something spectacular. Marie has found her formula and now she needs to create the drug. However, none of her colleagues even knew she was trying to accomplish this. Marie looks down, studying her work over and over, thoughts racing through mind. Her leg is bouncing up and down as she sits at her desk. Suddenly, Jim opens the door to her office, letting himself in.

"Ah! Marie how are you doing this morning?" he asked, almost mocking her.

"Fine. What is it you need? I am quite busy."

"Hey, now. Besides, what could be keeping you that busy?"

Bob is now standing behind him as he talks. A big smirk grows on Jim's face.

"This job could be stressful for someone of your … *nature.*"

Jim and Bob both share a laugh.

"You know, me and Bob just finished all of our work. You're slacking behind."

Marie had finished her work ages ago. What's keeping her busy is separate from her job. This was more. This was her future.

"You know," Jim continues, "me and you could always get dinner to make you feel better."

Marie's face shows obvious signs of displeasure.

"No," she says coldly.

"No?" he scoffs.

"No." she confirms. "Get out of my office."

"Ha! She's getting so mad," Jim says, looking at Bob, which is received with a chuckle before looking back at her. "You should really learn to not be so emotional. This is a place of work after all…" he says before he is interrupted.

Marie stands, her eyes meeting his. "Who do you think you are?" she says with an almost disturbing look of anger on her face. "Get out of my office now!"

Jim looked visibly startled. Marie had never gotten openly upset with Jim's actions. He would never admit it, but that face she made scared him in a way. He stands there for a few seconds, processing.

"C-come on," he says to Bob, taking a step back. They both leave, the office now silent before Marie falls back into her chair with a loud sigh, placing a hand to her forehead.

Marie had become obsessed. Every minute is now consumed by her work. Every meal, every walk, every drive, every moment, even in her sleep, her mind is racing of thoughts and ideas on how to better her work. Marie's appearance and attitude start to make an obvious change. Her blonde hair is now always in a messy bun opposed to her original different hairstyle every day normally consisting of a blowout, slick back bun, or ponytail. Her green eyes now have dark bags under them and look almost crazed. She still maintains proper hygiene despite these changes. Showering, brushing her teeth, or combing her hair, for some reason, allows her to enter deeper thought.

Marie is now at the stage of experimentation for her drug. She pulls into the parking lot behind her work like she has every day in the same car, with the same bag, and some newly added papers almost overflowing. Marie gets out of her car. It's about 3:30 a.m. and still dark. She makes her way to the back door of the building. She walks down the same long halls and into her lab. It's quiet. She's the only one there. Marie walks into her office and over to her desk, placing down her bag and taking out a single sheet of paper. The paper with the formula, circled, with the words next to it, "Our chance to be great."

She walks back into the lab with the paper in hand, placing it on the counter as she goes to what looks like a fridge. She opens said fridge. Inside lays different substances in bottles. Each one of these liquids is different. But to the human eye, you wouldn't be able to know the difference besides color; Marie herself made all of them. She grabs an electric, blue-colored liquid inside. She also grabs a purple one. After placing those down, she goes back over to the fridge and grabs another bottle. This bottle was different from the others. This liquid was swirling like a slow-moving tornado. It had yellow, orange and red—none of the colors mixed together surprisingly. She takes that bottle, placing it next to the others on the counter. She then pulls off a large piece of fabric like a blanket, revealing a large machine. It looks like something you would see in a movie.

Everything was translucent glass, except what resembles a box at the end. Tubes are running through everything. She grabs the blue substance and pours about a quarter into one of the tubes. You can see the blue sliding down the tube until it eventually reaches the box. She then grabs the purple and pours the same amount into a different tube. Marie takes hold of the swirling warm-colored substance.

She pours just a drop into a different tube. Like the first two, you see the colors even swirling in a droplet, never mixing, but sliding through before eventually reaching the box. Maries face doesn't express one specific emotion. She looks anxious, excited, scared.

Colorful, bright light radiates from the cracks of the box. A slight smile grows on Marie's face. She puts on a pair of long rubber gloves, opening the box. Inside is a new substance; she slides the container out from inside the box carefully. She places the container on the counter before turning around and grabbing a needle. Wait. What? Marie grabs the needle, dipping it into her drug.

"This is it," Marie says like she's still processing. "Life will be different after this."

Marie brings the needle to her arm and injects the drug into her vein. It's like she was just shot by a bullet. A color red flashes before her and she knows the drug was taking effect immediately. She grabs onto the table next to her for support. Her head throbbing as all the knowledge, all the answers, flooded her mind. She collapses, looking up at the ceiling.

"Being great never mattered. None of it does." Marie's face has a look of defeat. She lies there on the cold lab floor. No one would know what she had known. They couldn't. Marie stands, grabs the drug and chugs the whole thing, not a drop left. She collapses once more. This time, she would not get back up.

The newspaper boy rides his bike through a quiet neighborhood, throwing newspapers onto every lawn of every house he passes. The newspaper headline reads, "Woman scientist, Marie Watson, tragically dies due to unknown circumstances; police investigating."

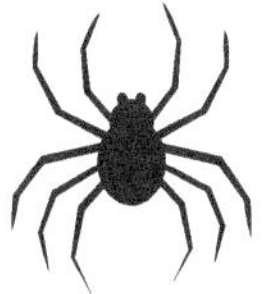

It's in the Walls

KELLEN WALSH

To begin this journal, about three hours ago, I was washing my dishes. In the corner of my eye, I saw a hand reach toward the light switch. My head spun so fast that I felt a sharp pain run through my neck. The dark silhouette wasn't there, so I went to investigate. Again, my assumption was correct. It was never there. I was confused and caught off guard. I went back to my chores, which leads us to this moment.

Creaking filled the halls of my house, and I'd just been sitting here. I live alone, so I didn't understand what was going on. I stood up to search for what was the cause of this racket. I creeped through the upstairs corridors and felt an overwhelming sense of uneasiness. I peered into every room. To my relief, I found nothing. So, I calmed myself to sleep.

Bang! Bang! Bang! the attic door rattled. I climbed out of bed and stared at the clock. It read 2 a.m. I clumsily stumbled around the house. I studied the silent, closed door at the end of the hall. I tiptoed to the door and wiggled the handle. The door slid open. I timidly peered around the attic and only saw dusty furniture and old Christmas supplies. Nothing; not a single hint of anything moving for a while. The dust on the ground was untouched. After that, I hadn't slept for days. I was exhausted, but I still couldn't even close my eyes knowing that might happen again.

Tapping occurred recently. It was just random taps all over. I couldn't for the life of me find the source of it. I started to look behind the furniture and in cabinets. Finally, I concluded that *it's in the walls*. I had to do something, or I would go crazy. When I was about to start my search, that dang silhouette started to pop back up. It also began to whisper in my ears. The thing was messing with me, and I just didn't know what to do. But I knew I still had to get in there. *In the walls.*

It's messing with me. I searched all over. The tapping just got worse, and I still can't sleep. I never believed in the paranormal before, but this may change some things. I've heard stories of people living in other peoples' homes. But I don't think that's what this is. It has to be a ghost. It has to. I'm just scared. I'm fearful of whatever demon lives in my house. Please help!

Banging noises keep coming from the walls. No longer the light tapping, there are now full bashes on the walls, like something is trying to escape. I'm hiding in my room with the door locked, hoping it won't get in.

I sat there until it mysteriously stopped. Out of nowhere, it was gone. I walked out of my room slowly and nervously scanned every inch of the hall. I swiftly proceeded to the kitchen. I examined it, every spot, but nothing. I swear I heard it. But still, there was no sign. I gazed at the wall at a massive hole torn through the wood and drywall. I stared at my work and thought about the past week. I thought about the shadow and thought about the tapping. I ran to my bathroom and rummaged through my cabinet, searching through bottles and boxes. I slumped down. I'm stuck here with nowhere to go. But suddenly, I heard a knocking at my door. I dashed through the halls, hiding behind every corner. I sneak myself to the front door. I stare through the peephole. My brother is standing at the door. I open the door, confused.

"What are you doing here?" I asked.

"I came to check on you. Let me in," he said.

"No. I'm busy. Go home."

"Okay. Wait! What happened to your…"

I slammed the door in his face. After that, my phone kept ringing so I had to get rid of it.

This monster is stealing my food! All of it is gone. I have no clue where it went. The banging has also gotten worse. Those deathly bashes are now going 24/7. I can't just go on like this. I have to do something. I ran to the shed in my backyard and picked up my grandpa's axe he had when he owned the home. I darted back inside. As soon as I walked in, the bashing started. I threw my axe at the area where the sound came from, and it just kept getting louder! I don't have anything. I run to my room, lock the door, and jump into my closet. The noise seems to quiet down, and I fall asleep.

When I got back, I picked up the journal and started writing this. *The walls are beginning to mold from a water leak or something. But the banging is still there. I ran to the kitchen to grab something. But when I climbed back up the stairs, a child was just standing there. It disappeared as soon as I looked straight at it. It was there. I knew it was. Also, my arm started to bleed a lot. It was as if I was slashed by a knife. I don't know. Everything is just falling apart. I'm going to go to sleep now.*

Nowhere safe now, the thing was in my room. It was whispering something. I don't remember it now. I'm hiding in my closet. It doesn't seem to know because the tapping stopped. I fear this child ghost thing more than anything else. It keeps on cutting or scratching me. I have like five marks on my arm now. It hurts so bad. I don't know how I'm going to sleep tonight.

A monster of some sorts is appearing in my dreams … *nightmares* is probably the right term. It just appears and screams at me and I'm so scared. To whoever reads this, please help me.

My arm is just soaked in a red layer of blood. The cuts don't stop. My fingers are also soaked in blood. I heard loud whistling and screams coming from my attic. I may go investigate, but my arms hurt so bad.

When I woke up, for the first time in a long time, the house was quiet. I couldn't even hear the normal creaks it made. For once, I had peace. Then, I heard a whisper in my right ear. I slowly turned my head. I saw it. I was face to face with a *thing*. I can't describe it. As soon as I looked, it was gone. I peer around the empty and destroyed room. A strange liquid was leaking from the walls, cracks on the ceiling and the floor. I knew I was stuck in my room. Banging starts at the door and then I heard whispers. I jumped up and slowly walked toward the door. I opened it inch by inch and saw nothing. The door to the hall was empty. So was the attic and kitchen. No signs that anything was ever there. I thought for a long time about the past month or so. How this all started and all the things that happened. I looked at my arms and they hurt more than they did before. I didn't care. I had a plan. I ran to my room and threw on a hoodie. I grabbed my car keys from the kitchen cabinets. I hopped in and turned the ignition. I drove to the nearby gas station.

"Gas prices are getting higher. Aren't' they?" asked some random guy. I just focused on what I was doing.

No distractions, I think.

"Did you hear me?" he added. I jumped in my car and drove off. When I got home, I threw the keys back on the moldy counter. I picked up the small gas canister I brought home. Banging and creaking filled the halls. I climbed the stairs and the monster appeared there. I screamed and darted back down the stairs. Bit by bit, I climbed the stairs. They feel like they lead to hell itself. When I reached the top, I stared around. Not to my surprise, it's gone. I dumped the heavy canister on the floor. I walked around the smelly liquid trail following me. The monster materializes in front of me. I stumbled backward. I walked toward it. Its dark eyes were glaring back at me. It screeches with a horrifying scream. It retreats to wherever it came from.

I carry the path of the gas outside. I pull a light from my pocket slowly. I stare at the metallic box. I flick open the lid. I light it and *boom!* The home lights into a gaping inferno. I gape at the flame eating away at the empty walls. Screaming fills the flames. I study the flames, looking for the monster that stalked me for so long. I walk around to my car and calmly climb into the driver's seat.

I drive in silence to a motel. I hand the man a twenty-dollar bill and walk to room six. I open the door and walk in. I lay down and stared into space with nothing really on my mind. I decided to go to a restaurant. I ate swiftly, paid and drove home. The evening felt too calm. I walked up to my room and opened the door. I get ready to go to bed, brush my teeth and drink a glass of water. I lie down and pull the sheets across my body.

But just then, I heard a light tapping. And, in the corner of my eye, I see a figure.

The Deathly Silence

HUYANNA PERDUE

The house slowly grew colder as each box Claire and her dad packed left the house. Within each box is a memory … a memory the two of them share fondly with each other. However, they also shared those memories with Lana Miller. The late Lana Miller was the mother of Claire Taylor and the wife of Jack Taylor. The now widowed father worried about his daughter all the time. Since Claire is deaf, she has always been the center of bad attention. The same town in which they lived was never short of gossip. So once Claire was born, it was like a celebrity showing up to town. She was picked on and laughed at, but the saddest thing is that she couldn't even hear them. So, they never stopped.

After Lana died, Jack and Claire decided to move out of the house that they were comfortable in. No more bad memories, no more ridicule, and no more pain. They were ready to start a new life. The girl never knew how her mother truly died. Her dad never explained it and has never brought it up either. So, Claire had to find out information herself. While packing one day, she found a letter her mom had written, and it was addressed to Claire's grandfather. Claire's grandfather lives far away from the town. Claire opened the letter. Within it was sentences upon sentences that made no sense to the fourteen-year-old girl. She sat there in silence and confusion. She reread the letter, picking up on details her eyes ignored. She somehow managed to understand that her mom was planning to leave before she died. It was almost as though she knew she would die. Lana had planned to take Claire with her, as well. Claire had kept the letter with her at all times. For reasons of speculation, she didn't want her dad to see this letter. The letter included secrets she knew she didn't want him to see. The details were surprising even to her. So, how would her dad react? He wouldn't. He would never see it.

As the boxes got moved into the large white van, Jack checked on Claire.

"How are you feeling about the house being empty?" he signed with his hands.

Claire smiled. "I'm scared." She signed and the smile became loose, showing the emotion she really had. "Do you think they will talk bad again?"

Jack looked away from his daughter's honey eyes. The painful glare she had stained his eyes with pain, as well. The next words weren't vocalized. They couldn't be. They were trapped within his throat. He looked back at her, giving her a sympathetic half smile. She nodded and continued packing her box. Claire got up and, a few steps later, she tripped. She glanced at the floor as a box of pictures had fallen out. Something caught her eye. A picture of both her dad and her mom was lying there. Her eyebrows cinched up together and her eyes stayed fixated on her mother's face. Happy as usual, her eyes sparkled with joy. But Jack was a different story. His eyes looked full of pain, and he wore such a forced smile. His dark demeanor made this picture look fake, like he was miserable. Claire grabbed the picture and tilted her head to the side, questioning her dad's expression.

Claire knew that all relationships struggle sometimes. What she didn't know was how badly her parents were. She couldn't hear the constant bickering. Even though she learned to read lips, she never thought she needed to read them with her parents since they were *supposedly* always open and honest. She couldn't hear if what they said to each other was with love or resentment. Her face contorted in disappointment. *This is the last thing I would hope to see*, she thought. Snatching her hand to her chest, sighed and pushed the picture into her back pocket. *What are you guys hiding?*

Within the house was one last room that had to be packed. This room was secure and locked. No one ever entered it. That rule was implied heavily by Jack ever since

Lana died. Only Jack was allowed to enter the room, and he only did so on occasion. The room was a couple doors away from Claire's bedroom and right next to the room Jack and Lana slept in. The little girl was never too suspicious of Jack and his room … until now. She searched far and wide for the key, in every corner, until she reached Jack's nightstand. It was open. Then, she finally found it. The bright golden key that connected to a string. She took it and ran quickly. Jack had left the house to check on the new place they would be moving to, leaving Claire alone for the first time in a long time. She knew Jack wouldn't trust her to be alone after this, but she needed to see whatever was in there. She rushed quickly to unlock the door. The lock was almost rusted and hard to budge. Once she got it, the door opened wide and so did Claire's eyes. The office had blood stain after blood stain. All she could see was red on the floor. The couch was practically covered in blood. Her eyes watered and her body pushed her forward.

The room reeked; almost as though depressed spirits roamed the room. She wanted to move, but her body remained motionless. When she finally regained as much sanity as she could, she stepped into the room. She found a desk on which held several pieces of ripped up paper. They connected together and she could make out the message.

"Dear Jack, we both know that this house is big enough for the three of us. But you no longer seem to make space for us. This house is now a confined space for you and your pity parties, and Claire and I will not be attending them anymore. You can't even genuinely smile in a picture with me. So, we will end this, so you can host an even bigger party for your emotions that overcrowd my and my daughter's life. She is coming with me to live with my father. You can stay here and enjoy whatever life you decided you wanted before I showed up, the life that I should never have been a part of. Goodbye, Jack."

Claire recognized these words. They were so similar to the ones in the letter she had; yet these ones were so much more painful. It was a goodbye, but clearly not Lana's last goodbye. Claire looked to her left, seeing all the mess that was made. There were two pictures almost exactly like the one Claire had in her pocket. Her mom's wedding ring was rusted and stained with the same red color as the couch. Before Claire could turn around and leave, there was a grasp upon her shoulder. It held her down, making her feet plant into the ground. Her body became stiff, and she felt a hard breath hit her head and neck. She blinked slowly and her stomach felt heavy.

Her mind drew blanks. Her breathing patterns were mixed and almost stopped. She turned, with the hand remaining on her shoulder. It was Jack. His face was hot and hung heavy. He looked mad, but calm at the same time. Claire's heart started beating so much faster.

Claire signed, "Dad, what is all this?"

He looked at her with scared eyes. "It's nothing. Claire, you aren't supposed to be in here!" he signed back to her quickly. She could tell he wanted to yell, but the words would have never got to her. Claire looked over the torn-up letter and back at her dad. His grip became stronger as his face drew up more. He was stiff, just like Claire. He started saying words. Claire almost got all the words, but he was talking too quickly.

"Why is there blood everywhere?" Claire signed and asked her dad.

Jack's look changed. He wasn't mad or angry, but he looked like his whole world came tumbling in. He could tell that the information he was about to share with Claire meant not only would he lose his wife, but also his daughter—just like the letter said.

His hand fell down and onto his face. He shook his head and turned the other way. He started walking away, in a quick motion with heavy feet. Claire followed quickly behind him. They sat down on the couch in the living room that hadn't been packed up yet. It took a while for Jack to say the words. So instead, he got up once again and found paper and pencil. He wrote quickly about what happened the day Lana passed. He looked over his messy handwriting and spelling errors. He handed the paper to Claire, turning away and beginning to pace.

The letter said,

Claire, your mom died three weeks after our trip on April 16, 1988. She had given me a letter with her goodbye. She came before she left to get you from your school, ready with a bag packed for you two to stay at least a week or two at your grandfather's until she could come back to get everything else. She said her goodbyes and I asked her to wait. We got into this huge argument about everything. I got so mad that I grabbed my stapler and threw it at her head. It knocked her out and she fell out on the couch. But I grabbed it again. I hit her multiple times. Blood rushed out of her head by the time I realized what I had done. I had to do something about it. I took her body to the backyard and started the fire pit…

The words traveled to the backside of the paper.

I burned her body and cleaned up all the blood I could. I took the letter and ripped it up and tried to hide any trace of anything. But that room was evidence that something happened to her. I went back outside to check if the fire died down. When it was gone, her ring was left over. I took that also. Luckily for me, the room had a lock. I locked the room and kept the key.

Claire looked at her dad with tears streaming down her face. He stopped his stride and looked at her.

"How could you do this?" she signed with her hands.

For the first time ever, she could hear. She couldn't hear anyone else's voice, but the one in her head. She screamed, which she never did. She got up, ripping the paper over and over. She pushed her father. Banging hard near his heart, she cried and hollered. She looked up at the man she knew as a monster.

"I'm sorry, Claire. I was miserable," is all she read from his lips.

She shook her head in disbelief. She looked toward the door. She ran, screaming. She wanted to get as far away from the man she so disappointingly called dad. She ran to where her feet took her—away from all the deathly silence.

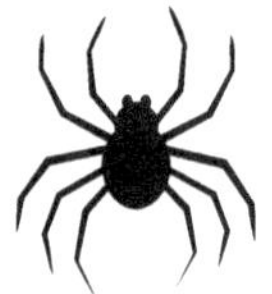

Kidnap

KINGSTON HOLIDAY-RICKS

One cloudy day, I woke up to get ready for the writing club. I stretched out my arms in my bed before getting up. I went straight to the bathroom to clean up. I started by brushing my teeth. It only took me ten minutes to do all of the things I had to do upstairs. Afterward, I ran down the stairs.

I yelled, "Good morning, everybody!"

"Good morning," my brother said.

"Morning," my mother said.

"What's for breakfast, mom?" I asked.

"Some bacon and eggs."

"That sounds good, but what about some sausage with it?"

"No, no, mister. Eat what I have made for breakfast."

"Alright."

"Also, you might want to hurry up because it's 9:30 and the camp starts at 10 a.m. Do you want me to drop you off today?"

"Naw, I will be fine. Plus, there's nothing to be worried about."

Those words that I said will be something I will remember for the rest of my life. As I got ready to head out, I had to play one game of 2k24 before I got my bike and went to my camp. It took ten minutes to play one game of Blacktops 1v1 and soon realized it was 9:45. I had to go before I was late. I got my key, snack, drink, notepad, phone and bike lock. I closed the door and went to the garage. I grabbed my bike and rode off. I only lived down the street from where my camp was being hosted. So, I could ride my bike when my mom said it was okay. As I got to my first turn on the road, I had to cross from one sidewalk to the other. I saw my friend Jayden on his trampoline and stopped to talk to him for a minute or two. I finished the conversation and got on my bike to keep going.

I heard my phone ring and I had to check. I grabbed my phone out of my bag and checked it to see that someone's bike had been missing for four days, and it was finally found at a random gas station. I was confused why I got the text. I looked up to see things that will change my life forever. I saw a guy in a car doing circles in a parking lot by some apartments. The driver hit the gas and went up to the curb I was on. To my surprise, he started to get out of his car. I was scared due to the fact the man was coming up to me quickly. Luckily, I got back on my bike and hid behind a house in the neighborhood. As I hid, I saw the car drive into the neighborhood. This was my opportunity to get away. So, I got back on my bike, but my tire got stuck in some dirt.

"Come on, you stupid thing! Can you get unstuck please?"

It took me a minute to get it out. After I got it out, I rode my bike to the school, taking precautions as I rode. As I got closer, I saw the car and the person. But this time was different. He was posted on the corner of a neighborhood where my friend Atharva lived. He started up his car and drove. He hit a 180. I rode my bike faster than I ever had. I didn't want to look back, but I had to. Luckily, I did because my friend Atharva was right there on the sidewalk with me.

"Atharva! Atharva!"

"Yo! What's up?"

"Dude, I'm so scared bro!" Tears of relief and fear rained down my face.

"What happened? Why are you crying?"

"There's a guy in a black Honda chasing me! He was just posted on the corner of your neighborhood. He chased me here and did a … there he is right there!"

As I pointed behind Atharva, he looked back to see a car chasing us.

He said, "Dude, we have to go NOW!"

As I looked over his head, the guy was driving as fast as ever. He was mad over something, and we got scared. We hopped back onto our bikes and quickly got to the school. We didn't even look to see if cars were coming. We just booked it to the school. We got to the school, and we just had to cross a road to get to the doors and security. We looked both ways and there was no car coming. We crossed the street and went to the bike rack. We jumped off the bikes and put the bikes on the rack. Atharva didn't have a bike lock, but I did. So, he waited for me to put on my lock. We walked in and acted like nothing happened. When we got through security, Atharva looked at me, confused.

"Why didn't you tell them what happened?"

"Because I'm going to tell my mom first so she will know. She is the first person to talk to before anyone else."

"Okay. Well, I've got to get to my class. Good luck getting in contact with your mom."

"Thanks."

When I walked down the hallway to get to my class, I felt a little bit of relief and safety in the hallway. It was quiet, too. I was still scared though. It also felt like I had to cry, but I had to stay calm. I didn't want to cry and embarrass myself. When I got to the room, I sat down and looked up to take a quick breather. Then, I looked down and looked around to see if there was anyone looking at me. I texted my mom to tell her what happened.

I texted, "Mom, something happened. I was riding my bike and a guy started to do circles in a lot. I was suspicious and he got closer. His car hit the curb and he got closer. I was lucky that I was on my bike. I went into my friend's neighborhood and hid behind a house. He went into the neighborhood also. So, it was my chance to leave. But my tire got stuck. Eventually, I got out. But when I got back on the path to the school, he was posted on the corner of my friend Atharva's neighborhood. He drove toward me. I sped toward the school, and I looked back. I saw Atharva and I told him what happened. Then, the car chased us again. This time, we made it to the school and we walked in. I still don't know what to do!"

"Call me!" my mom texted.

"Wait! Wait!" I texted.

As I tried to stop her, the phone went off. I wasn't going to answer the phone, so I asked one of the teachers to go to their room and safely talk to my mom about what happened.

"Hello?"

"Mom! I don't know what to do! I was minding my own business, and then he decided to chase me and try to get me!"

"Okay! Look, have you talked to anyone about it other than me? Like a teacher or security?"

"I was going to talk to security, but I didn't know if you wanted me to tell a teacher or something like that."

I cried a little harder.

"Go tell an adult. Afterward, do you want me to come pick you up?"

"Yes, please."

I hung up the phone and went to tell the teacher. The only thing that kept me calm was the fact I was crying walking into the class. So, when I walked in, everyone turned around and looked at me to see what was wrong. I told the whole class what happened. At first, some people started laughing. But when I finished my story, they all were surprised and shocked. One of the teachers decided to take me to the front of the school and tell the administrators and security. I got to the front and told them what happened. I first talked to the administrator, and he took me to security so he could see what the guards would say about all of this. This time, both me and the administrator told them what happened. They said this was higher than what they could have done, so they wrote a report about what happened for the Oakland County Police Department.

Throughout the conversation with the security guards, I cried even more. My cousin came over and talked to me to see what happened. When I stopped hugging my cousin, my phone buzzed, and my mom texted that she was outside. So, I told the administrator, and he walked me outside. My mom watched me come out. So, I ran toward my mom and gave her a big hug. After the administrator told her what happened, I went home and relaxed to relieve my mind of stress.

But I will never forget that day.

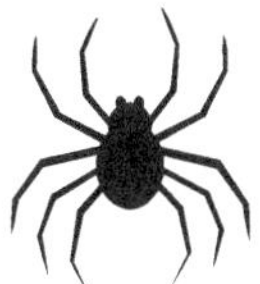

It's All in Your Head

SHANIA LOPEZ

I'm sitting in my room on the squeaky wooden floor. It's wintertime here in California. I have hated the winter ever since I was a little kid and my mom died in a drive-by in her car, which made her car fall off a bridge. The funeral was mid-winter during a storm.

I lost track of time and realized it was almost 2 a.m. I just sat there, staring out the window, looking at the moon. Suddenly, I saw this creature. It was a tall creature with dotted red eyes. I thought it was because of all the stuff I'd been smoking. So, I just shook it off and went to the bathroom to brush my teeth and get ready for bed. But as I was getting ready for bed, I felt something breathing down my neck. I turned around to see what it was. Nothing was there. I finished up getting ready and went straight to bed.

I woke up to the sound of my alarm. I got up and changed my clothes for school. I did my hair, fixing my ocean wave curls. My mom always wanted to chop it off since it was down to my waist and was hard to manage. I put on my earrings and my white Air Forces.

"Camila, ya es hora de la escuela! You're going to be late for school if you don't hurry up!!" my dad said.

"Okay! I'm coming! Sorry!" I yelled.

When I got to school, I got to my class and sat down in my seat next to the window. As the teacher was teaching the class, I zoned out. I started drawing. I heard a voice that sounded like my mom's. I turned my neck to see where that voice was coming from. Nothing was there. *I shouldn't think anything of it*, I told myself. It was the end of the school day, so I walked home. Maybe it would help me keep my mind off of things.

When I got home, I laid down on my bed, staring at my ceiling. It was so quiet that you could hear a pin drop in my room. No one was home since my dad went to work. I decided to take a nap to kill some time. When I woke up, it was already 6 p.m. I went downstairs to get dinner. I made myself a sandwich. As I was putting the tomato on the sandwich, I saw that face flash in front of me. It was the face I thought was nothing, but I was wrong. I let out the most terrifying scream and ran into my room. I sat down on my bed, shaking. Everything went blurry, my heart beating fast. I didn't know what to do. I sat there waiting and telling myself that everything would be okay. I passed out. When I woke up, I went straight to bed. I couldn't go out of my room after what I saw.

The next day when I woke up, I went straight to my dad to tell him what happened.

"Dad, can I tell you something that happened?" I asked in a shaky voice.

"Just make it quick, Camila. I have to go to work."

"Yesterday in the afternoon when I got home from school, I saw this creature or figure. I didn't know what it was…"

My dad interrupted me before I could say anything else. "Camila, you're just crazy. What's wrong with you? You didn't see anything! You should just get some sleep!" he yelled at me.

"But I really did see it! I swear!"

"Just stay home from school at this point. I don't want to hear another word about that creature or whatever."

"Okay, Pa. I'm sorry." I went to my room and sat on my bed. I realized maybe all of this wasn't just in my head. *Was I going crazy? Should I tell someone else? What if they don't believe me? Maybe I should just keep it to myself. It does sound kind of crazy. I'm just going to go outside and take a walk. Maybe that would calm me down.* I went to go on a walk outside, but something felt different, as if I was being watched. But nothing was there when I looked around. Maybe it was because of what happened yesterday. I decided to go home. When I got home, I got my backpack and got out my homework. Since there was nothing else for me to do, I couldn't stop thinking about that creature. *What could it be? Why am I seeing these things? Am I dreaming? I wish all of this could go away, including this creature. Maybe I should find out what it is. There has to be something about it. I can't be crazy. I know what I saw. I should just wait for my dad to get home and tell him more about it. Maybe that's why he didn't believe me.*

As soon as my dad got home, I went straight to him about it. "Dad, I promise I'm not making this up. I saw a creature with red dotted eyes. It was like a shadow. Why don't you believe me? I really did see it and, at school, I heard mom's voice. I'm not lying. Please believe me."

"Camila, are you crazy? That's not real. You were probably just dreaming or something. That can't be true. And don't bring your mom into this. Okay? Because she's gone. You're a psycho. Stop telling me about all this nonsense! It's not true. It was just a nightmare. Now leave me alone!"

I ran to my room. *Why won't he believe me? I know what I saw and I'm not crazy.* I slammed the door. I stared at my window, hoping I would see that thing again. I had to know that I'm not crazy. There it was! That shadow with red eyes appeared! But something was different. It got closer and closer. It was standing right in front of my window. I yelled and backed up, hoping it would go away. But more of them came out of nowhere. It somehow got inside and was crawling right in front of me. I started banging my head against the wall, hoping all of this was just a dream. I went unconscious.

I woke up in the hospital. I saw my dad.

"Mija, are you okay? What happened to you?" he asked.

"I just tripped. I'm fine," I mumbled.

"Well then, be careful! You scared me!"

"Sorry."

I couldn't tell him the truth since he would think I was joking again and get mad. So, I just stayed quiet.

A week later when I left the hospital, I thought everything was okay. In the hospital, there were no voices, no creatures. I was fine. *Or so I thought*. I decided to go to school again after all that. I shouldn't be missing school. It's not like there's a reason for me to go. I don't really know anyone, even if I've known them since middle school. It's already my senior year. I guess I never really knew how to interact with anyone. But I guess I did have some friends before until they moved. I really don't like anyone here anyway. At the end of the day, when school ended, I walked home since everything was okay now.

As I was walking home, I felt as if I was being watched again. I looked around and I was being watched. It was the shadow on all fours coming toward me. I ran as fast as I could. When I got home, it was right outside my door when I checked. I locked the door and ran to the basement, hoping it wouldn't find me. I stayed there until my dad got home. I was calmer knowing that my dad would be home with me. I wouldn't have to worry about that thing that was "in my head." At night, I had my dad cover my windows and have my door open just in case anything happened.

In the morning when I woke up, my dad told me that he had to go to work and that he would be back early. I didn't want him to go since I was scared of being home alone now. When he left for work, I heard my mom's voice again. When I looked around, I saw her outside behind my window. But it wasn't really her. It can't be! *Who is this?* She disappeared. I stared at the snow falling from the sky as she disappeared. *What happened?*

I sat there staring at the window. Something came back, but it wasn't just my mom. It was the shadow grabbing my mom and ripping her apart until it was just her body and head. All her body parts were on the floor. The necklace she used to always wear was on the ground covered in blood. I cried. I didn't want to live through this anymore.

The Creepy Circus

MIKEY QUINN

It was a nice Saturday morning in the summer of 2025. Mikey was excited because it was his brother Nikey's 14th birthday party today. His parents trusted Mikey, who was fifteen years old, to watch over his brother and his friends. His parents would be going to Detroit for dinner and leaving the boys alone to have their party. Vikey arrived first with a small gift. Then, Tikey arrived soon after. Mikey's parents ordered pizza to be delivered for the boys to eat. There was also a fruit platter because Mikey loved blueberries. They also had a blue moon ice cream cake for dessert. His parents made him promise they would sing Happy Birthday to Nikey.

The party got started with some music and dancing to their favorite rapper, Lil RM. Nikey decided to open Mikey's present first. He ripped off the paper and opened the box, which contained a PS6. Nikey was so happy!

"Mikey, this is awesome. Thanks, bro!" Nikey exclaimed. Then, he opened the gift from Tikey, which was an iPhone 17. Vikey gave him some green grapes because he had no money to buy him an expensive gift. They all laughed so hard until they cried because they thought it was a great prank.

Mikey was setting up the PS6 in the living room with the help of Tikey and Vikey. Nikey was in the kitchen looking out the door glass when he noticed a man standing outside. His face was burned. It almost looked like he had a smile permanently burned onto his face. He was tall and had big muscles. He was wearing a bright yellow shirt with just a smile on it. He had short brown hair and no shoes; he only wore dirty white socks. When Nikey looked at him, he smiled and revealed his rusty teeth. Nikey turned his head for a second. When he turned to look back at the door, the man was gone.

Nikey called out to Mikey, "There's a creepy guy standing outside!"

Mikey yelled back, "Don't go out there!"

But it was too late. Nikey walked out the door. When he did, he felt a pain in the back of his head. Someone had knocked him out with a stone and put him into a garbage bag.

When Mikey was done setting up the PS6, he walked outside to look for Nikey. Mikey called to the other boys,

"Come outside!" They walked outside and saw the note hanging on the door. The note had a picture of the old circus.

It read, "I got your friend! You want him? Try to fight me or he dies."

The boys knew about the old circus that was fifteen miles away. It had been abandoned since 1969. There had been a fire and one person died. It had never been rebuilt and it was locked down for no one to enter. Mikey decided to drive his dad's blue Lamborghini to the circus. They decided to take some bats with them.

The circus was rusty, dusty, and musty. The ground was dirt and rocks, so it made it noisy to walk on. The tent was yellow but after years of neglect it had fallen to the ground. The rides had become rusted and worn down. Most of the things there were broken down. The police had put fences around the circus to keep people out. There was a long, gray driveway with a smile painted on it.

When the boys arrived, Mikey broke the gate using the bat. They walked in and saw rusty rocks with blood on them. They continued to walk to the big rollercoaster. There was a real clown that grabbed Tikey, who was following behind the boys. Vikey heard Tikey scream and said, "They got Tikey!"

Mikey looked back and there were twenty clowns standing behind them. Vikey started fighting them. He told Mikey, "Go save Nikey and Tikey! I got this!"

Mikey looked at Vikey and said, "Okay! I'll go save my brother and Tikey."

Mikey ran to save his brother and friend. He saw a sign that had a picture of a house. He realized that the house was where the killer lived. He kept running and saw a campfire burning. He saw Nikey tied up with a string. He was next to the fire and looked like he was being cooked. Mikey ran over to him and grabbed him. He had found some gasoline and threw it onto the fire. Mikey untied Nikey and said, "We still have to look for Vikey."

Nikey informed Mikey, "It's too late for him. He's gone. We have to get out of here." Mikey and Nikey saw the killer standing next to the fire.

Vikey fought the clowns, but there were too many of them. He tried to run away, but the clowns got him. They beat him up. He couldn't make it out in time when the fire began to spread. The fire spread and there was a gas tank next to them, which exploded, killing them all. The killer made it out on time. He ran into the forest to hide. Mikey and Nikey ran back to the car and drove fast to get back to their house. Their mom and dad were already home. Mikey told them that there was a killer. They told them what happened to Vikey and Tikey. Mikey told them that Nikey needed to go to the hospital. The mom and dad took Nikey to the hospital. Mikey was left at home alone, so he tried to clean up the mess from the party. He fell asleep while waiting for his parents and brother to come home.

When they arrived, Nikey went to brush his teeth. On the glass was written with blood, "I will get you again!"

In the morning, they ate cereal and pancakes. They went to the graveyard to bury their friends. When everyone left, Mikey was the only one left at the graveyard. Mikey saw the killer next to a tree in the forest. He ran away from the killer. His dad was in the car waiting for him, so he hopped in his dad's car. Mikey told his dad that he saw the killer again in the graveyard.

Mikey said, "Drive, Dad! He's coming!"

The dad drove quickly, trying to get home as fast as he could. Later that night, Mikey's mom and dad had an important dinner event to attend. So, they left the boys home alone.

Mikey brought some friends over because he didn't want to be alone in their house anymore. Aikey and Rikey came over with a beach ball, pizza, fruit and drinks. They convinced Mikey to go to the beach. Nikey decided to join them, as well. He was scared and didn't want to be alone.

They headed to the beach to relax. They were having fun eating and swimming. Nikey went to the bathroom and saw that there was a lot of blood going toward the bathroom on the ground. He grabbed his bat, just in case.

He walked into the bathroom and into the stall, where he saw blood and water. He saw a person's head. He ran out of the bathroom to Mikey and told him, "There's a lot of blood by the bathroom!"

Mikey said, "I don't believe you! I need proof."

Nikey showed him where he saw the blood and head. They both ran out of the bathroom to their friends and said, "Let's get out of here!" There were a lot of gray clouds and blood in the ocean. They ran to the car and drove back home. Their mom and dad had not come back home yet. Or so they thought. Instead, the boys found them dead in their room. They didn't see Rikey behind them. So, they went downstairs and saw him dead. The three boys ran back to the car.

The boys went to the police station. They told them everything that happened. The police kicked the boys out of the station.

The police officers told them, "Never come back! You're just trying to rob us."

They went back to the car and drove home. They buried their parents and Rikey in the graveyard. Mikey went back home, brushed his teeth and went to bed. Nikey was in his room. He was looking in the mirror and saw the killer was directly behind him. Nikey ran around the room, screaming for help. Mikey got up and ran to Nikey's room, but the door was locked. He kicked down the door. Mikey grabbed the killer and threw him out the window. The killer fell. However, when the boys looked out the window, he was not there. Mikey covered the window with a piece of wood and tried to fix the door. They called the police and made a plan to capture the killer and send him to jail. The plan was that the police would be there hiding, waiting for the killer. Aikey, Mikey and Nikey would be at the circus to call out to the killer. They were waiting for him to show up, but they saw a ghost. The killer grabbed Aikey, and the police came out. They grabbed the killer and took him to jail. He was arrested for all the murders and trying to kill the boys. On the way to the jail, the killer tried to break the bars on the police car. The police car crashed, and the killer escaped from the car. He ran back to the circus. The police looked for him but couldn't find him anywhere.

Seven years passed without seeing the killer or hearing of any other murders. Mikey and Nikey decide to go back to the circus grounds. The circus had been fixed. It had reopened and it was filled with people. Everyone was having so much fun. There were several rollercoasters, carnival games and food. Nikey and Mikey rode one of the rollercoasters. They sat in the front seats.

When they looked back, the killer was sitting in the back row of the rollercoaster. He had a creepy smile and was waving at Mikey and Nikey.

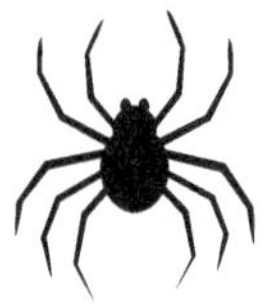

The Invisible Girl

JORDYN S. HILLIE

"Alright, class! Have a great fall break and happy almost Halloween!" Mr. Crimshall said, happy that we were all leaving his classroom.

"Hey girls," Jade said, coming to the lunch table that all her friends Imogen, Peyton and Rose were seated.

"Hey!" they all said in unison.

"So, girls, remember I told y'all the plan about the sleepover?"

"About that we can't do it at my house anymore?" Imogen asked.

"What! Why?" Rose asked.

"Because my parents are not going out of town anymore."

"Wait! We can do it at my house. My brother can cover for us," Peyton said.

"That's perfect!" Rose said. Jade noticed Imogen looked sad and mad at the same time.

"Alright. We will all meet at Peyton's house at let's say 7 p.m.?" Rose asked. Rose was the leader who kept everyone together. And she loved it!

"Deal!" Peyton said.

They all left and went home.

"Hey, Imogen! Need a ride?" Jade asked.

"Sure."

"Hey! You okay? You looked upset when we had our best friends meeting."

"Yeah. I'm fine."

Jade knew something was making her upset, but she didn't want to make her even more upset. They dropped Imogen off to pack for the sleepover. When Jade got home, she got her ghost detector and ghost communication speaker.

"Mom, I'm gonna be late!" Jade said.

They finally arrived at Peyton's house.

"Alright! Bye, mom!" Jade said.

"I know, mom! Bye," Imogen said as she was arriving at the same time. Jade waved at her, and they walked to the door together. Before they could knock, Rose opened the door, scaring them both.

"Hey, Jade and Imogen! You got the stuff, Jade?"

Peyton's house was huge. It looked like a five-star hotel when you first walked in. They had a huge golden chandelier and all white carpet.

"Okay. My parents are gonna go to sleep around ten, tops!" Peyton said.

"That's perfect! While we wait, let's check and see if we have everything," Rose said.

"Check. Check. And check," Jade said.

"Let's talk about the backstory," Rose said. "So, it's about the old Robinsons."

"Oh, yeah! The mother's name is Nadia," Jade said.

"Right. And the father's name was … wait. Does anyone know his name?" Peyton asked.

"Forget it," Rose said.

"The person we should really be talking about is Merida," Imogen said.

Everyone started to get chills.

"We need the backstory," Imogen said.

"But we don't know the backstory. All we know from the old newspaper is that Merida killed both of her parents, then killed herself," Peyton said.

"You're right, Pey," Rose said. "What's your problem, Peyton? Why do you always have to correct me?"

"Hmmm. I don't know. Maybe it's because you're always wrong."

"Girls, can y'all not fight today?" Rose asked.

"Okay. Operation is a go. We leave now," Peyton said.

They snuck out the window.

"Okay. We can take all four of my bikes," Peyton said. "Hurry! Get on."

They got on the bikes. On the ride, it got colder with every second.

"Good thing we brought blankets," Rose said.

They arrived at the house, which was black with tree branches all over and two big doors. Most of all, the house was huge!

"How are we getting in again?" Rose asked.

"My Bobby pin," Jade said.

They entered the house. It was cold and dark.

"Good thing we have flashlights," Peyton said.

"Where are we sleeping?" Imogen asked.

"In Merida's room," Jade said.

"Let's put our stuff in there and explore," Rose suggested. They put their stuff down and split up into groups. Rose and Jade needed Peyton and Imogen to get along, so they put them in the same group.

"Y'all, check upstairs and we will check down here," Rose said.

Peyton and Imogen went upstairs. They went into the parents' bedroom. They saw knives with fresh blood on them.

"Oh, no!" Peyton yelled.

"What is it?" Imogen asked.

"I-I think someone is in the house with us."

Imogen and Peyton went downstairs to look for Jade and Rose.

"Jade! Rose! Where are you?" Imogen yelled.

"Down here!" a voice yelled from the basement. Imogen and Peyton went downstairs where Merida was kept. Chains and a table with a story book were in the middle of the floor.

"She wrote her own stories," Peyton said.

"But to who?" Imogen asked. When they were looking through her story book, they found something that gave them chills.

"We have to tell Jade and Rose about this," Imogen said.

"No! We need to keep this a secret!"

"Imogen! Peyton!" Jade yelled.

"Here we come!" the girls said, running up the stairs. "Find anything?"

Rose said, "Uh … actual…"

Imogen interrupted and said, "Nothing! We found nothing."

"We can finish the rest tomorrow. Let's go to sleep," Jade said. They headed upstairs. To their surprise, they found their stuff moved around.

"Did anyone move our stuff?" Jade asked. They all shook their heads.

"Ummm … we did find fresh blood in the parents' room," Imogen said.

Peyton looked at her angrily.

"I'll go look. Y'all go to sleep," Jade said. They started to fall asleep. But before they did, Imogen was praying.

"Lord, please protect us tonight. Maybe give us some clues on how to find Merida or save her soul. Amen."

They all slowly fell asleep while Jade was downstairs looking for that fresh blood. However, she never found it.

Jade came back upstairs and went straight to sleep. Time went by. It was now 3 a.m.

Bang!

They all jumped up.

"Ugh! I had the weirdest dream," Jade said, holding her head.

"Wait! What was your dream about?" Imogen asked.

"It was Merida's backstory," Jade said.

"I had that same dream," Peyton said.

Had they all had the same dream? What could it be? What did Merida do to her parents? Or what did her parents do to her?

"What was your dream like, Imogen?" Rose asked.

"It was about Merida telling a story in that story book we found downstairs."

"Wait! What story book? Peyton said you found nothing!" Jade said. "Who lied?"

Rose blamed Imogen for nothing because she was always on Peyton's side, no matter what.

"So, who's lying?" Jade asked.

"It's Peyton. She told me not to say anything."

"Why do you lie, Imogen? I'd never do such a thing," Peyton said.

"That's why we shouldn't have put her in this friend group because she's a liar," Rose said with a mean face.

Imogen wasn't always a part of the friend group.

"I'm going to the bathroom," Rose said. She wanted to turn the shower on just to clear her head. As she did, steam was building up on the mirror. She breathed in and out, thinking about if she should apologize to Imogen. Rose looked up at the mirror. There was steam with a message. It said, "If you can't believe in one friend, don't believe another."

"What is this?" Rose screamed as she got scared.

She came out of the bathroom frightened. "I think Merida's watching me … or *all* of us!" Rose said, breaking down.

"Where did Imogen go?"

"She left. She said she didn't belong because of you and Peyton double teaming her."

Jade yelled, "Oh, well!"

Peyton didn't really care what Imogen felt. Imogen was just now leaving at 4 a.m., trying to open the door. But it was locked. She pulled and pushed, but the door would not budge. Imogen stepped back slowly and bumped into Merida's father.

"AHHHH!"

Imogen ran back upstairs, screaming in shock.

"What is it, Imogen? What happened?" Jade asked. She was the only one answering Imogen. After all, she was the only one not mad at her. "Oh, my! Imogen, you're in shock!" Jade said, feeling bad for her.

"It was Merida's father! He's alive," Imogen managed to get out, still frightened.

"Wait! What?" Peyton asked as she hopped up from lying down.

"I-I saw him. He was clean with dark hair and was really tall, just looking down at me."

"I thought you were gone," Rose said, irritated as she was coming back from the bathroom.

"I saw Merida's dad."

"Sure. And I saw her mother." Rose could sometimes be a little sarcastic about different things. "Let's communicate and see what we can get from any ghost."

They got the communication ghost speaker and started asking questions. Merida was talking to them.

"Merida, why is there a story book?"

"To tell them the truth." Merida's creepy voice was frightening.

"What truth?"

It went quiet. Then, she said something that gave everyone chills.

"The people in the walls."

"What does she mean people in the walls?" Peyton was not listening until now.

"Let's go get that book," Imogen explained.

They all went downstairs and got the story book. They read the stories aloud. *The Girl Stuck in the House* was the first story.

"This is about her," Jade said while reading the book about how she went for revenge. "They locked the girl when she talked to people through her windows. She never went to school because of her face?"

Rose was confused. They were all confused.

"We need to free her soul today and now," Imogen stated.

"She's been locked up for a disability," Jade said.

She didn't have a top lip. Her parents wanted her to get surgery, but she didn't want to. So, they locked her up.

"They didn't want to be seen with her!"

The girls went back upstairs to prepare to free her family's soul … or maybe just hers. They managed to open the door. They grabbed their stuff and the ghost communication speaker.

"We are now freeing your soul. We saw your story and how you've been in here your whole life."

It was eerily quiet. Then Merida whispered, "Thank you." They all get chills.

"Ugh! Can we leave now? I'm ready to go back home," Peyton complained. "Yeah, but we need to talk—like a meeting," Jade demanded.

"Imogen felt like she didn't belong because of you and Peyton," Jade said.

"I lied when I said we didn't find anything. Imogen was telling the truth," Peyton said.

"Rose, do you have anything to say before we leave because Imogen felt invisible like Merida did?"

"I'm sorry, too, that I said all those things about you. You should be in this friend group. I was wrong."

"Good! Do you accept these apologies, Imogen?"

"Yes, I do. Thank you, guys."

The girls were all now best friends. Merida is now free … but what happed to Imogen seeing Merida's father?

The girls forgot all about him and moved on.

But the father was still an unsolved mystery.

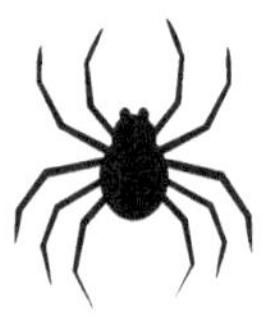

Cycle of Rebirth

EVAN SMITH

It's a rainy night on a Sunday. A young, teenage boy named Bryson Sinclair came into the kitchen of a two-story house and opened the freezer, hoping for an easy night snack to chew on. He found a box of pizza rolls. He breathed a sigh of relief as he happily put ten pizza rolls on his plate, entered it into the microwave, and waited for a few seconds. He stood by the kitchen cabinets, patiently waiting. Suddenly, he heard an annoying alert sound coming from the living room. He walked in and saw his dad lying on the couch and looked at the TV. The screen had a black background with white text overlayed on the screen.

"Emergency alert system! Local Oakland County issued! There is a serial killer on the run. We advise you to remain locked inside of your homes until further notice."

Bryson was confused. A random killer, roaming on the streets, seemed crazy at first. But he walked up to the front door to make sure it was locked. Then, Bryson checked the windows and the back door.

All is good, he thought.

Beep, beep, beep, beep!

The microwave was done. Bryson took his plate of pizza rolls with him up the creaking stairs.

Creak! Creak!

"Mom and Dad need to fix these stairs eventually, or else they will break open." He reached the top of the stairs and walked through the hallway. He passed the bathroom and his parents' bedroom. He noticed frames with pictures of himself when he was younger, particularly photos of him when he was a boy scout. He reached his bedroom and opened the door. He was happy to finally relax on his bed, munching away on his pizza rolls. After he finished, he missed the trash can when he threw the crumbled-up plate, and he laid back down.

Outside Bryson's house, little did he know that a figure was standing on the sidewalk of Wayfare Lane. The figure had an all-black outfit with an overshadowing hoodie and a red mask. The mask had cartoon eyes that had dilated pupils, a long nose and a mustache. The coldness of its breath was visible. The look of the figure and the way it lurked is what made it unsettling. It seemed like hours passed, but really, it had only been a few minutes. The breeze of the air stormed through Bryson's window since he'd forgotten to close the window before relaxing on his bed.

Creak!

The sound of the creaking stairs once again made a noise. Although the irritating noise could be heard from everywhere in the household, Bryson, however, didn't hear it. He was in a deep sleep. Bryson felt a sudden change in the air of his room. Something was off. Something wasn't right. He opened his eyes as he looked at the ceiling and slowly pointed his eyes down at his door. The door was still closed it seemed, but he saw something in the far corner of his room.

The bone-chilling red long nose mask was there, lurking, as if it was watching him, staring at him like an owl. Bryson rubbed his eyes to get a clearer look, but the figure disappeared. Suddenly, it reappeared on top of Bryson's bed.

Bryson tried to scream for a moment, but the figure covered his mouth and gut punched him in the stomach with a sharp blade. The sound of Bryon's guts repeatedly gushed as Bryson finally kicked the figure onto the wall. Bryson stumbled over to his desk, barely keeping himself up. He reached for his phone. But the figure quickly threw the blade onto Bryson's hand. Bryson's hand was stuck on his desk. He was unable to scream anymore as blood overflowed from his mouth. He limped over his desk. The figure walked up, took the blade out of his hand and slit Bryson's throat.

Everything went black. When he came to, Bryson's vision was blurry, and his ears were ringing. Finally, his vision and hearing became clear. Bryson realized he was on his bed, like usual.

What happened? Bryson thought to himself. Just a few minutes ago, he'd vaguely remembered what happened last night. Bryson looked down at his floor and saw blood stains on the carpet. At this point, Bryson realized that he somehow had survived. He pulled up his shirt and there were no stab wounds on his chest nor on his hand.

Resurrection?

New Life?

Rebirth?

He didn't understand. Bryson was confused, worried, scared and paranoid.

A few hours passed, and Bryson came home from school. He ignored his parents in the kitchen and went upstairs. He walked into his room. The blood stains were slowly fading away, but he noticed something else. He walked in front of his window and saw the figure that was there the night prior. He was standing in the bushes with the same unsettling stare that was there before.

Bryson ran downstairs to lock the door but was interrupted by his father.

"Bryson," his dad started. "Your teachers have informed me that you have not been participating in classwork for a while. What's going on?"

Bryson looked to the right. "It's nothing." Bryson said as he locked the door.

"Have you looked in the mirror today? You look pale," his father continued. Bryson touched his face and walked upstairs. Bryson went into the bathroom and turned on the shower. After he closed the shower curtain, he saw an overarching shadow behind him. Bryson froze in fear. The water of the tub flowed up as the shower head continued spraying water. Bryson didn't know what to do, but he stood in hopes that it wasn't the figure from last night. The water of the tub spilled onto the floor. Bryson went to open the curtains. Suddenly, a hand grabbed him tightly on the wrist and dragged him into the water. Bryson was helplessly drowning in the tub and eventually gave up trying to move as he lost his breath.

Beep! Beep!

The sound of an alarm echoes in Bryson's ears. Bryson groaned and turned over in his bed before he quickly sprung up. Huffing and puffing, he found himself losing control of his breath. The feeling of dying and instantly coming back alive felt like swallowing disgusting food and vomiting it back out. He looked down at his hands, which were growing more pale. Bryson heard the sound of the news from the TV downstairs. He walked up to the couch and looked at the screen.

"Ten found dead at Oakland Park."

This park was only a few streets down from Bryson's house. He kept listening.

"Citizens have spoken about the killer by the name of The Blood Devil."

Bryson looked at the calendar on his phone and realized that a day had already passed. But, for Bryson, it went by so quickly between that one night and right now.

I have to find a way to break this cycle, or else, I'll just go… insane! Bryson thought. As the hours passed, the more anxious Bryson got.

5:05 p.m.

Bryson walked down the sidewalk as he got back from shopping. He figured out a plan to trap and kill The Blood Devil. Bryson thought this would break the cycle.

He heard footsteps from behind and turned around. He saw The Blood Devil running at full speed. Bryson ran as fast as he could with two bags in his hand. He went through the front door but didn't have time to close it. He ran up the creaking stairs, but they broke beneath him, trapping him with spikes of wood piercing his leg. Bryson screamed in agony as The Blood Devil ran and put Bryson in a chokehold. Bryson screeched and begged for air. However, Bryson thought, *Today has to be different. I need to escape this curse!*

Bryson put his other foot against the steps and launched himself and The Blood Devil backward, landing on the ground. The Blood Devil was the only one who was really hurt. Bryson got up slowly due to his injured leg and threw a punch at The Blood Devil. Bryson threw another punch. The Blood Devil caught it and kicked Bryson over the couch. They launched over the couch, but Bryson was gone. The Blood Devil turned around and got hit with a frying pan as they both fell to the ground. The Blood Devil got up and tackled Bryson, picking him up and slamming him headfirst. Bryson started bleeding from his head as he watched The Blood Devil take off its mask, with blood dripping out of it. Bryson looked surprised.

Bryson reflected on his Boy Scout days when they were doing a group activity at a creek. Bryson was assigned partners with a boy named Devon. The group activity was simple, a scavenger hunt where they had to find different tools around the creek and hurry back to the camp. There was one specific rule though:

No swimming or walking near the creek!

Apparently, there were alligators, hippos and other creatures in the creek. As Bryson and Devon walked back to the camp, they heard a boy screaming. They ran over there quickly to see a boy trying to climb back up from the creek.

"You guys! Please! Pull me up!" the boy begged.

Devon went to pull the boy up. "Bryson, I need help!"

He struggled for a bit. But it seemed like it was working … until something pulled the boy down in the water, along with Devon.

"Bryson! Help!" Bryson was scared and didn't know what to do. So, he ran away.

Back in the living room, Bryson was staring at Devon for the first time in five years. Devon had a huge scar on his eye as he looked down on Bryson.

"You left me there to die, which cursed me in a cycle of rebirth. After that, I vowed to kill you, which also cursed you. That's why you're in a cycle."

Bryson's eyes slowly closed as he bled out. From Devon's eyes, Bryson disappeared until the next day. Devon left the house and waited for Bryson to be reborn again.

The next day, Bryson was already awake. He felt guilty after what he had done to Devon, but he had no other choice but to break the cycle. He set traps down in the basement and exited the basement through the shaft door that led outside. A few hours passed and it was nighttime. Bryson stood outside, waiting for Devon to appear. A figure walked from the corner of the sidewalk and walked up to Bryson.

"It's him," Bryson whispered. Bryson ran and so did Devon. Bryson ran to the shaft door outside his house that led to the basement.

Devon opened it and walked down the steps. He tripped over a string and fell down on a sticky goo on the ground. Devon tried to move up, but Bryson turned on a bunch of nail machines, aiming toward Devon. A bunch of nails stabbed Devon to the ground as Bryson walked up to Devon.

"I-I'm sorry ... Devon," Bryson said slowly. Devon launched himself toward Bryson, but Bryson stabbed him in the head with a kitchen knife. Bryson, thinking he'd won, looked down at a blade in his chest.

Bryson stumbled and collapsed on the ground, ultimately dying.

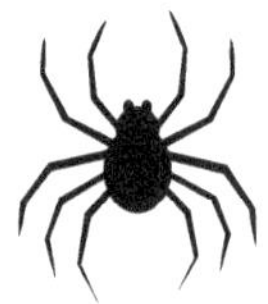

A Nightmare to Remember

JANYIAH HOLLOMAN

The three main characters in this story are a 13-year-old girl named Dream, Meranda her mom, and Evan her dad. One day, Evan went to work. While he is at work, Meranda killed her daughter because she was born deaf. Meranda thought Dream would be like all the other kids—normal and fine. But because she was born deaf, her mother was mad. Dream was only in seventh grade at the time. Just that quickly, Meranda had forgotten that there were cameras in the family room. Unfortunately, she forgot to unplug them.

This was her dilemma. All the video footage was there. Meranda couldn't lie about the murder or what happened to the Dream. A few hours later, Evan comes home from work. He walks in and he sees that Dream was dead on the floor.

He yells, "Meranda! Come here now!"

Meranda entered the room slowly.

"Did you do this to Dream?"

"No! I would never!"

But by the look on her face, Evan knew she was lying about something.

"Oh really? Let me check the cameras then!"

Evan gathers the footage of what happened. He couldn't believe that she would lie to him. Evan calls the police officers and explains everything that happened.

"Officer, when I got home, I saw my kid, Dream, on the floor! I also checked the footage of the cameras that I put in the living room. My wife Miranda lied to me! She killed her! I can't believe she lied to me!"

When Evan got off the phone with the police officers, the police rushed to the scene. Once they reviewed the footage, they took Meranda away in handcuffs.

"I'm not going to jail!" she screamed.

"Oh, yes you are, ma'am! You committed a crime against your daughter and that is twenty years in prison minimum! Anything you say or do will be used against you in the court of law."

The police put Meranda in the back of the police car and drove away. Abilene came to the house to take Dream to the closest hospital. Evan follows Abilene there. Hospital staff took Dream into surgery immediately. They soon came to let Evan know that Meranda had only given Dream a concussion. Meranda had shot Dream in the head, intending to kill her. Dream spent six months in a coma. During that time, it was touch and go. Evan thought he would lose Dream many times during those six months.

Meranda had unfortunately tried to break out of prison multiple times. She finally was able to escape using a sledgehammer. Soon, family members got word that Meranda was out. Evan's mother went crazy. She immediately hit the streets looking for Meranda. She couldn't believe Meranda had done this to her grandchild.

"I'm going to kill her!" she told Evan.

"Mom, calm down please!"

While most of the family gathered at Evan's house, Meranda made her way to the hospital to see Dream. Meranda was worried because she didn't know if she would run into any family at the hospital. Just that quickly, she forgot she had to be in court soon with Evan. When she left the hospital, Meranda decided to head to her house. She didn't know that the police were already on the lookout for her. When she got to the house, Meranda could tell that all of their family members were there. Meranda slowly opens the front door and sees all of her family sitting there, looking angry.

Evan's mom yelled out, "I'm going to kill you!" as she noticed Meranda at the door. Evan's mom grabbed a knife from the kitchen and charged Meranda. She quickly stabbed Meranda in the stomach and Meranda dropped to the floor. The family wanted to protect Evan's mom, so they buried Meranda's body in the backyard.

A few months later, Dream comes home from the hospital. All of the family was so happy to see her. They all took loving care of her while she was at home resting from her recovery. Months later, the family regretted what they'd done to Meranda. Evan's mother looked like a beautiful girl with long black hair and green eyes. She was slim with a thick waist. Evan was skinny with hazel eyes, and Dream had long black, silky hair with really light brown eyes. The family was all so beautiful. They lived in Alabama, and it was always hot there. The family constantly had to go to the store and buy a lot of water and food.

When Evan and his mother showed up at court, the lawyers asked a lot of questions. Lawyers asked for proof of what happened to Dream. Evan handed his phone to the judge so he could play the video footage.

The judge said, "So, you lied to Evan about what happened?"

Evan's mother said, "Yes, I did, your honor."

"Why did you lie about what you did?" the judge asked.

Evan's mother said, "I don't know. I didn't want to go to jail."

"Well, you're going to go anyway!" the judge said before slamming the gavel.

"Your honor, I'm still going to keep my daughter, Dream, right?" Evan asked.

"Yes, you are still going to keep custody of your daughter, Dream."

"Thank you, your honor."

The court dismissed. Evan's mom was sentenced to jail and Evan was free to go home. When Evan got home, Dream was happy to see her father. Dream didn't even ask about her mother or grandmother. She wanted to forget all about what happened. It was like a nightmare that she couldn't get out of her head. She often dreamed it was happening all over again. It was a nightmare she couldn't shake. The trauma was forever etched in Dream's mind of what her mother had done. It was a nightmare she would forever remember.

The Clowns

NYLA JOHNSON

It was a dark and stormy night. I was home alone, and I was sitting on the couch watching TV. Suddenly, I heard a noise coming from upstairs in my parents' room. My parents, who had been gone for two weeks, were in Florida for a vacation and my brother was only God knows where.

I live in a three-story house. The house is white on the outside, and most of the walls are white inside the house. Some are yellow, and my room is pink.

At first, I thought it was my brother who was upstairs getting something out of my parents' room. But when I looked on my phone on the Find My app, he was at someone else's house. He had been gone since this morning. When I texted him, asking where he was, he told me he was sleeping at a friend's house. When he sent me that text, I was scared. I knew my parents weren't home. So, because I wanted to be brave, I went upstairs to check it out.

As soon as I got up there, my parents' light was on in their bedroom. I knew that the light was not on before because I went up there earlier to get my charger for my phone. Then, out of the corner of my eye, I saw red curly hair. This is when I got terrified. Instead of running, I went in more to see if I was delusional. And there it was: a six-foot clown standing there with a smile on his face and a knife in his hand.

Its face was painted white. Its mouth was painted red, and its eyes were painted red in the shape of a long diamond. It had on a Pennywise costume, like he got it from Party City or something.

I hid in the pantry to call my parents, my brother, or 911. However, my phone died as soon as I turned it on. Then, it found me. I started running all around the house, thinking that maybe if I ran around enough times, he would get tired and pass out. I believed if I prayed hard and God protected me, it might just happen. I wanted to go back to the family room to quickly grab my charger so I could run upstairs in my room and call someone. While the clown was still chasing me, I grabbed my charger and ran upstairs to my room and locked the door.

I plugged in my phone so I could charge it. Then, all of a sudden, I heard the clown run back downstairs and go outside. I thought he had finally given up and left me alone. But I was wrong. When the clown went outside, it found a ladder and went around back to where my room was and set the ladder up against the house. When I heard the ladder on my window, I knew that the clown hadn't left yet. I opened the window and there he was, climbing up the ladder. At this point, I was begging God for my phone to hurry up and turn on so I could call the cops. But it wouldn't turn on. It was almost like the clown had turned off the power.

But how is that possible? I asked myself. *The clown was inside the whole time. Unless…* I heard a bang outside my window interrupting my thoughts. It was the clown. I unlocked my door. By the time I was downstairs, the clown had made it into my room. I heard it talking to someone. It sounded muffled, but I managed to hear what the clown was saying.

"She got away! I need to find her before she calls the police!" the clown said.

"Yeah! You can't go back to jail, dude. *We* can't go back to jail. Luckily, I turned off the power." I could hear the other person on the speakerphone.

Then, I opened the door to the basement of the house so I could hide. The door creaked loudly, unfortunately. I knew he heard it because the clown stopped talking to the person on the phone and I heard him say, "I'll call you back. I think I found her."

I ran downstairs, looking around. Then, I saw the perfect hiding place. In our basement, we have a place under the stairs where we put our Christmas trees, ornaments for the trees, wrapping paper and suitcases. So, I opened the door as quickly as I could. I got on one of the tubs of ornaments, closed the door, and sat down in the back of the Christmas trees so that the clown couldn't see me. I had just enough room for my legs so I could lie down inside the closet. I heard the clown's footsteps above me as I held my mouth, trying not to make any noises. I heard him looking around, throwing stuff everywhere. Then, he opened the door.

At first, I thought it was over. But he didn't see me. I took a deep breath, whispering, "Thank the Lord." I got out of the closet and ran back upstairs so I could run to my friend's house. We had to call the police. I ran upstairs quietly so that the clown couldn't hear me. I closed and locked my door quietly, closed my window, locked it, and packed everything I loved in my suitcase. Then, I grabbed my backpack. I put my computer, my computer charger, my phone, and my phone charger, some water and snacks (good thing I had those in my room) and my headphones in the backpack. After I finished packing, I unlocked my door. However, I still kept it closed. I opened the window and climbed down the ladder. I went around the back of the house to get my bike out of the garage. I didn't know where the clown was, but I thought my escape was a success. Good thing my dad had a big enough basket to put on my bike for my suitcase.

I attached the basket to my bike, put the suitcase in it, then put on my backpack and rode my bike to my friend Tyler's house. As I pulled my bike out of the garage, I saw another clown in the car, staring at me.

"Uh oh!" I screamed. I rode my bike fast down the big hill. The other clown started the car and drove toward me. I turned the corner, and the clown was right behind me. I turned another corner and went straight. I turned the second to last corner before I got to Tyler's house. I went straight for a couple of seconds. Then, I turned the last corner. It was a ginormous hill, so I just cut through Tyler's yard, parked my bike in the driveway, and ran up to the front door. I banged on the door.

Tyler came out in his pajamas, asking me, "What's wrong?"

"A clown is right behind me! I don't know what I did for them to come after me! But can I please come inside? I have nowhere else to go."

Tyler told me to come inside, and he let me spend the night. After I went inside, I told Tyler, his mom, and his siblings what happened from the start. We called the police officers and told them what happened, and they sent police to the location. They were able to arrest both of the clowns. Then, the police officers came to Tyler's house and told us, "Thank you for calling us. We have been looking for these guys for a long time. They are going to be locked up for good."

"Thank you, officer," Tyler's mom replied.

"No problem!" one of the officers said. "Young lady, you are very lucky that you called us. They could've killed you!" After the officer left, we called my parents. The good thing was that they were going to be back tomorrow. Then, I spent the rest of the night terrified because of what happened. However, I managed to make it through the night.

In the morning, me, Tyler and his little brother Justin played on the trampoline until my parents told me to come home. When I came home, everyone wanted to make sure I was okay.

"So why did you break in? It was a little girl!" the police officer said.

"Because I wanted to!" the clown replied.

"Hey! Do not raise your voice at me! And that little stunt that you did with your friend is gonna give you both life sentences!"

"Whatever. Are we done with this conversation?" the clown asked the police officer.

"Yes! Hey, boys! Get him out of my office!"

"I just want you to know one thing: my friend and I *will* escape! Just … you … wait!"

Then, the clown was taken away for sentencing.

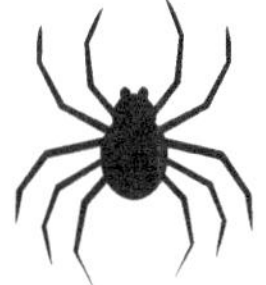

Sweet Flower

STAR CONTRERAS-GUZMAN

2010 September, 12

Dear Diary, today is my birthday. Mom and Dad are still fighting, I can hear them talking about me. And lucky me! Dad didn't come to my room last night! :) Happy birthday to me! Love, Roselyn.

I drew a little bunny at the end of my words before I closed my diary and pushed it under my bed as I held onto one of the limbs of my stuffed bunny. Getting off the floor of my bedroom, I approached my bedroom door and peeked through the crack.

"Gosh, Harold! It's your daughter's birthday! Can't you put that bottle down for even a day!?" Mom yelled at Dad as he raised his empty beer bottle at Mom.

"Don't tell me what to do, woman!" he yelled back, clearly drunk, before he smashed the beer bottle over her head.

Mom stumbled over her feet as her body collapsed to the ground, a pool of blood surrounding her head. Covering my mouth, tears welled up in my eyes. Dad stepped over Mom's body, grabbed a cold beer from the fridge, and disappeared into the living room. An overwhelming number of feelings filled me like a glass full of water.

I took a careful step out of my room while sobbing silently so Dad wouldn't hear me. I dragged my stuffed bunny behind me. Approaching my mother and kneeling on the ground next to her body, I shook her and pleaded for her to wake up.

"Mom … wake up! Please!" I whispered desperately as I shook her shoulder, brushing her hair out of her face as I held her head.

The blood from her head stained my hands as I hopelessly tried to wake her up, believing that she was still alive. Unbeknownst to me, she wasn't. Tears kept falling, no matter how many times I wiped them away, the blood staining the area around my eyes. After what seemed like hours, my tears finally stopped coming. I was too exhausted even to move. I simply rested my head on her stomach and closed my eyes to sleep, holding my bunny to my chest.

As the next morning came, the sun rose and shined through the windows of the dark home. The sun shone in my eyes as I rose from my slumber, sitting up before staring down at my mother. She wasn't breathing. Exiting the kitchen, I entered the living room as I spotted my blackout-drunk father sleeping on the couch, the television still playing in the background. I stood there watching him, thinking of his actions and how he treated Mom. The more I thought of what he did, the angrier I got.

"I have to get rid of him!" I thought as my face scrunched up. "The kitchen. It has knives," I said under my breath before walking back to the kitchen, taking a chair, and dragging it behind me to the counter where the knife block was. I climbed on the chair, reached for one of the knives, took it with me back to the living room, dragged the dining room chair with me, and sat it next to the couch where Dad had passed out. I got back in the chair before stabbing the knife right into his chest repeatedly before finally pulling out the bloody knife from his chest. I stared at his now dead body before I reached a hand inside his chest, cringing at the feeling of his insides. I pulled out whatever I could get my hands on and threw it on the living room floor. I looked at the mess I had created, gagging a bit before leaving the knife on the chair and going back to the kitchen, back to Mom.

"I did it … you won't have to worry anymore; *we* won't have to worry…" I murmured as I sat next to the corpse that used to be my mother.

2016, November 18

Renie rested her cheek on the palm of her hand, boredom catching up since there were barely any cases to work on. Just as she was about to fall asleep, her partner, Nikolas, a Minotaur, opened the door to her office and stepped in, his hooves hitting the wooden floor of her office with a few beige-colored folders in his hands.

"Don't go falling asleep now, Shelley. We got a new case on our hands," he said as he placed the folder in front of her. The sound of his voice jolted her awake, glancing up at him from her seat before looking down at the folder. There was a picture of a dead man with his insides surrounding him in the shape of a flower in the folder, as well as another close-up picture of the empty hole on his chest. The file of the dead man contained where the man lived, what he did for a living, etc.

"Woah! I guess we have another killer on the loose…" Renie exclaimed, astonished at how the poor man was brutally murdered, holding up the folder to take a closer look.

"That's not the only one, unfortunately. They made their way to the side…"

Nikolas sighed as he placed two more folders, the two other victims being two fauns. They had also gone through the same fate as the other man who was presented in the previous folder. She looked up at him with her eyebrow arched before sighing.

"The fantasy world? Oh, God…"

Arriving at the first murder scene, Renie and Nikolas stepped out of the car. The area was surrounded by yellow caution tape that said 'POLICE LINE! DO NOT CROSS'. The alleyway reeked with the smell of decaying flesh and blood. Renie covered her nose as her face scrunched up while Nikolas talked with another policeman.

"Good evening, Officer Rowan. Do you think that there are any cameras around this area that can be checked?" Nikolas asked as he looked down at the other officer while holding the files to the murder victim, checking the name of the victim.

"Yes. There's a bank facing over on the other side of the alleyway that has cameras."

Officer Rowan nodded his head before Nikolas thanked him for the information and walked back over to Renie. Walking under the caution tape and stopping next to Renie in the alleyway as she stared down at the body of the dead man, Officer Rowan marveled at how the organs made a flower around the poor man.

"His name was Denis Goodwin. Had a wife and two kids…"

Nikolas put his hands on his hips, huffing slightly, his breath visible in the chilly air.

"And the bank over the other side has cameras. So, we can probably find out who is finding all of this out and made this gruesome mess."

He continued glancing at her.

"Gruesome sight indeed. Who even does something like this? Making a flower out of his organs…" Renie muttered as she rubbed her temples, crouching down next to the body, examining the cut hole in his chest before she noticed something glisten inside the man's decaying body.

Putting on a surgical glove, she slowly reached a hand inside his chest, pulled out a short bloody knife, and held it in the air before standing up straight and dropping it inside a small transparent bag held by another police officer. She breathed in a sharp breath, the cold air making her teeth hurt momentarily.

"What a surprise…" she murmured as she looked around to talk to Nikolas. However, he was nowhere to be found. He'd probably went to the bank to check the cameras to see if they had anything that might lead them to the killer.

Nikolas sat with the security guard in the security room as they checked the footage from the cameras outside the bank. While the footage from a few nights before played, he saw someone enter the alleyway.

"Stop! Go back a few seconds!" Nikolas exclaimed as he pointed at the screen before the footage was replayed and paused at the moment before the black hooded person entered the alleyway. The security guard zoomed in on the person. They could make out that the person had a porcelain mask covering their face.

After collecting the footage, he thanked the security guard for his time before exiting the bank and going back to the scene, meeting back up with Renie. Renie had her back turned to him as she was talking off the bloody surgical glove she had on, hearing the sounds of hooves approaching her, knowing it was Nikolas as she looked over her shoulder.

"Found a knife in Mr. Goodwin's chest. Sent that to get checked," she asked as she turned and faced her partner. She let out a breath as she rubbed her hands together to keep warm.

"Killer has a porcelain mask. That's all I could get. And by what I saw, our murderer didn't have anything to cover their tracks!" Nikolas responded, tilting his head slightly to the side. Renie crossed her arms.

"Next stop: Gremlins Forest…" she muttered as she nodded her head a bit.

Upon arriving in the fantasy world, they passed a few other magical creatures who were very paranoid about the deaths of the two fauns. The closer they got to the next murder scene, the stronger the stench of blood and rotting flesh got. The area was restricted and surrounded by a magical force by the witches and wizards to not traumatize other magical beings in the realm.

"It stinks in here…" Nikolas said as he covered his nose and shook his head while they entered past the magical border. Renie nodded in agreement to his words.

"Of course, it's going to stink. You expect it to smell like candy and honey?" Renie asked sarcastically as she shoved her hands in her coat pockets.

2016 November, 26

It was early in the morning when we got the results of whose fingerprints were on the knife used to kill Mr. Goodwin. *Roselyn Justine*. Nikolas was left in shock when they read the name of the fingerprints. Renie, however, was glad to find out who caused these deaths, but was confused by her partner's reaction to the new information.

"Nikolas, is something wrong? Why do you look shocked?"

"That's my niece. Roselyn is my niece," Nikolas said troubled with a look of horror on his face.

Night with Black Hood

YULIIA CHOBIT

It was a rainy evening, and Yulia was very bored. She decided to invite her friends from high school, Isabella, Noah, and Jordan. After twenty minutes, there was a knock on her door. She was mesmerized by the delicious smell of pizza, which was brought by her best and very funny friend, Noah. Isabella was her gorgeous friend who had long, soft hair, and good designer outfits.

She opened the door and was happy she could be alone. A few minutes later, her mom called and said her friends could stay overnight because she could see them on the cameras. They were all happy and started to party.

But at some point, they received a message on their phones saying, "Look out the window!" At first, they thought it was another friend playing a joke. But no. It was a message from a stranger named Black Hood. They didn't pay much attention, but Jordan was very curious. So, he looked out the window. He saw a tall man dressed all in black with a big black hood, a big spine, and long arms visible from behind his long coat. Jordan was scared and called his other friends. But they did not believe him.

A few minutes later, Isabella was very hungry. She went to the kitchen to see if there was any more pizza. There was nothing. She decided to go down to the basement.

During this time, Yuliia was ready to dance. She also decided to check the camera to see who it was and where it was. Nothing strange was happening, but they didn't know it was already in her house.

After a few minutes, they took a break from dancing and couldn't find Isabella.

"She probably ate your whole basement," Noah said.

"Probably," Jordan confirmed.

"Guys, it's funny. But I think some of us should go check her out," Yuliia replied to Noah's joke.

After five minutes, Noah and Jordan decided to go. But Yuliia said that she was just checking the cameras.

When they were going down the stairs, they felt a coldness on their hands and something very strange. At the same time, they heard scary sounds, as if someone was following them. They stopped to check, but there was nothing.

"Can you hear it, too?" asked Jordan.

"Yeah. But I think it's just because it's raining outside and there's a mile-a-minute wind," Noah replied.

Yulia shouted at them from the room, "Go away, you cowards!"

They finally decided to open the door. Rather, *Jordan* did. They tried to quietly go down to the basement and check on Isabella; everything was fine with the cameras. As they were loading, she noticed that some of them were missing. Most of the cameras in the basement were not working anymore.

Yuliia shouted, "Come upstairs soon!"

There was no answer. She heard something coming up to her room. She was excited and thought it was her friends. But it was the Black Hood. She soon ran out of the room and down to the basement to see what had happened to her friends. When she came downstairs, she saw her friends lying dead, and Yulia cried hard, but quietly. She didn't understand how it all happened so quickly, quietly, and without any marks. She still heard the monster getting angry and decided to escape through the exit. It was a little hole in the pit. There were spiders and stuff near the exit because she hadn't used it for quite a while. But she realized that it was better to be dirty than dead.

She tried to get through the hole and realized that today's pizza was extra. She slowly drove it so the monster wouldn't hear her. When she got all the way through and wanted to leave, she heard the door break, and someone grabbed her leg. She shouted loudly, but it was useless. She lived in a new house and there were no neighbors. Yuliia read where her old house was and wanted to run to it, but a nail was stopping her that she'd got caught on. Yulia felt someone very quietly approaching her leg and wanting to catch her. She lost her bearings and soon crawled out with her torn pants. She cried extremely hard and ran with all her might, falling several times. She still wanted to reach her mother in her old house.

When she was running, she looked back and saw that no one was there. She didn't dare go back to that house. She walked as fast as she could because she was very tired. She'd been thinking about how he did it so quietly and quickly. It is literally impossible. When she came to her old house, she told everything to her mom with a lot of tears and shaking hands.

"Don't worry, my little girl. Everything is alright!" Mom said.

"Mom, my friends. They, they, they are … *dead*," Yuliia replied.

"Oh, my God! It's okay. We will fix everything, and we will find this Black Hood!" mom whispered.

My mother decided to call the police. They also had cameras. When the police arrived, they asked a lot of questions, but Yuliia could not breathe. When the police looked into all the stories and took fingerprints, there was nothing but Yuliia's. Of course, she explained everything to them.

"I don't understand what happened. There was a lot of blood and this monster…" replied Yuliia.

"I'm afraid we don't believe that. I think it's time we went with you to the police station!" replied the sheriff.

When they arrived, Yuliia started to hold back, and her mother had to intervene.

"You have no right! The child has just survived the deaths of her friends and you are taking her to the police station!?"

"Ma'am, we understand everything. We have a lot of evidence that your daughter committed this murder!" the police officer replied.

When Yuliia came out of the restroom in the police station, the police and the sheriff gave her a lot of evidence that she did it. She explained to them that it was not true.

The police officer didn't care. Of course, they didn't believe her. So, they sent her to a psychologist.

"How do you feel?" the psychologist asked.

"I'm fine! Let me go!" Yuliia screamed as she responded to the psychologist.

After this incident, the psychologist realized that it was not worth continuing to communicate with her, and it would be better if she went to a psychiatric hospital. She reported this to the police, who agreed with the psychologist's suggestion. When Yuliia was packing her things, she thought she would be released. But she did not know that her mother had already signed a contract for her granddaughter to live in a psychiatric hospital. The police picked up Yulia and took her to the nearest hospital.

"And where are we going?" Yuliia asked the police officer.

"Home." Of course, he had to lie to her.

When they arrived, Yuliia immediately wanted to run away, but she was caught by police dogs and police officers.

When they brought her to the ward, she fell asleep and did not want to talk to anyone. She stayed there for a week. Her mother decided to visit Yuliia and tell her something. Yuliia did not want to hear her mother. She wanted to hit her mother, but her hand did not rise.

"My dear daughter, I will serve you. I beg you!" said her mother.

"Okay. I'll listen to you. But you only have ten minutes," Yuliia replied.

"Thank you. The sheriff gave me a lot of evidence about you and your fake murder. I believe you, but they don't. If I said I wouldn't sign it, they would send you to your grandparents' home and me to prison," her mother said, dropping her tears on her food.

"Okay, mom. Don't cry. I understand, and I don't want to hurt you. But can you leave me alone now?" said Yuliia.

Yuliia ate a home-cooked meal and it was time for bed. She didn't want to sleep. But because she was crying, she fell asleep. That night, she dreamed about the Black Hood. She dreamed about him killing her mother. After that night, she didn't dream about him again. Nothing happened to her mother, and no one heard anything more about the various murders of the Black Hood.

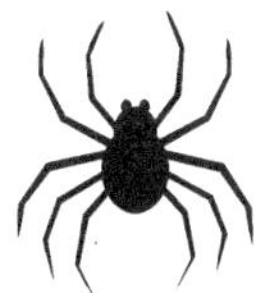

About So It Is Written

We help entrepreneurs write the ONE book that will expand their reach and get them to SIX figures in record time!

As the leading content curators for authorpreneurs and entrepreneurs, So It Is Written is best known for helping them package and leverage their expertise into a bestselling book, which amplifies their brand, accelerates their paydays and attracts bigger opportunities!

Let us help you brand in excellence as an author and entrepreneur so you can develop multiple streams of income from just ONE book!

Call us at 313-777-8607 today or email info@soitiswritten.net for more details about our services. We look forward to collaborating with you to make your project one of excellence!